MAGICAL MUSEUM

BAGHDAD AND BEYOND

WEAM NAMOU

HERMiZ
PUBLiSHING

Library of Congress Cataloging-in-Publication Data
2025919293

Namou, Weam

The Magical Museum
Baghdad and Beyond
(Middle Grade Fiction)

ISBN
978-1-945371-18-9 (paperback)
978-1-945371-19-6 (eBook)

First Edition

Published in the United States of America by:
Hermiz Publishing, Inc.
Sterling Heights, MI

10 9 8 7 6 5 4 3 2 1

CONTENTS

The MAGICAL MUSEUM

BAGHDAD AND BEYOND

CHAPTER 1

The Magical Arrival in Baghdad

Stepping through the arched entrance of the Baghdad and Beyond Gallery felt like entering a valley. The faint scent of jasmine mixed with mint chai, and the soft melody of a qanun filled the air. They greeted me in Arabic, and I greeted them in return.

"This is breathtaking," Helen said, admiring the walls painted in rich gold and turquoise, mirroring the Tigris and Baghdad's iconic domes.

"It's like a window into the heart of Baghdad," I said, watching her face light up. In her polka-dot dress and radiant joy, she seemed years younger.

The children traced their fingers over the intricate Arabic calligraphy that flowed across the walls, weaving poems and proverbs passed down through generations.

"Read this one!" Zaya called to Mary.

"He who strives, achieves," Mary read aloud, "and he who walks the path will reach his destination."

1

Lola, ever the dreamer, pointed to another inscription:

"إذا غامرتَ في شرفٍ مرومٍ فلا تقنعْ بما دون النجومِ,"

"If you venture into a noble cause, do not be satisfied with anything less than the stars," she read. Then, looking up at me, she asked, "Does that mean we're star material?"

"Definitely," I said. "Though some of us shine brighter than others," I teased, glancing at Mr. Yatooma, who was admiring his reflection in a glass display case.

"Abu al-Tayyib al-Mutanabbi," Helen read the name next to the inscription. "Who was he?"

"He was one of the greatest Arab poets," I said. "Born in Kufa, Iraq, in 915 CE, he came from a humble family but claimed noble Arabian roots. He lived with Bedouin tribes, mastering pure Arabic, and later became a famous court poet, especially for Sayf al-Dawla in Aleppo. His nickname, 'Al-Mutanabbi,' or 'the would-be prophet,' came from a time when he briefly claimed to be one."

"Wow," Helen said.

"Al-Mutanabbi Street in Baghdad is named after him," I added. "It's the city's historic hub for books and ideas—a place full of poetry and history."

The children's eyes lit up, captivated by the story.

At the center of the room, a glowing map of Iraq stood illuminated, its cities marked by tiny golden lights. Baghdad pulsed brightest of all.

"Whoa," Zaya said, stepping closer. "This place is next level."

"It belongs with the moon and stars," Lola said dreamily.

"This is beautiful," Mary whispered, clutching her notebook, her eyes already scanning the room for details to sketch.

"Isn't this where you were born?" Mr. Yatooma asked, leaning in like he'd uncovered a national secret.

"Yes," I said with pride. "Welcome to the city of the Abbasid Golden Age—a place of learning, culture, and resilience."

"Ms. Weam," Mary began, flipping through her notebook, "didn't you write in one of your books about sleeping on rooftops here?"

"Yes, that was so memorable—"

"But didn't you also say the flies woke you up in the morning?" she interrupted, curious.

"Some landing in people's mouths?" Zaya added, his eyes sparkling with mischief as the kids burst into giggles.

"Well, you see…" I stammered. "That's… part of the authentic Baghdad experience."

"Authentic?" Zaya smirked. "Sounds more like Baghdad's 'early morning alarm system.'"

"Let's focus on the gallery," I said, gesturing around with forced enthusiasm. "It honors the Chaldeans who built their lives in Baghdad and other cities across Iraq, leaving their mark on history."

"Were there a lot of Chaldeans in Baghdad?" a child asked.

"Yes, there were," I said, relieved to shift topics.

"Baghdad was a melting pot," Mr. Yatooma added, stepping beside me with a wide grin, his energy bubbling over. "Muslims, Christians, Jews, and people from all over the world lived side by side. And guess what, kids? It wasn't just a center for trade and politics—science, literature, and art thrived here like nowhere else."

"Children, did you know people called it the 'City of Peace'?" I asked.

"City of peas?" Zaya said, squinting.

"No, peace," I said, laughing. "Although a city of peas would be easier to manage. No wars, just… butter."

The kids chuckled, but Helen tilted her head thoughtfully. "It seems full of fighting in recent years."

"Well, things have changed over time," I said. "But once upon a time, in 762 AD, Caliph Al-Mansur founded Baghdad and called it *Madinat al-Salam*—the

4

City of Peace. It became the Abbasid Caliphate's capital and one of the most important cities in the world."

"Peace and butter," Zaya muttered, earning another round of giggles.

"That's pretty awesome," John said, high-fiving Zaya.

"Children, listen up," I said. "While the Abbasid period was a golden age for Baghdad, Chaldeans continued to thrive here long after. They built churches, schools, and businesses, becoming an integral part of the city's fabric."

Just then, the soft glow of the gallery lights seemed to shift once again, drawing our attention to a new section. The words "Echoes of the Chaldeans" shimmered in both Arabic and Aramaic.

"Looks like the next part of the story is waiting for us," I said, gesturing toward the display.

From the back of the group, a small voice asked, "Oh, is it waiting? How do you know?"

I paused, meeting the child's curious gaze. "Because stories like these never stop calling to those who are ready to listen."

Echoes of the Chaldean

CHAPTER 2

Echoes of the Chaldeans

The warm glow of the gallery grew richer as we moved deeper into the exhibit. Ahead, a tall display came into view, its title *Echoes of the Chaldeans* etched in both Arabic and Aramaic.

"Here," I said, gesturing toward the display, "we revisit the ancient roots of the Chaldeans before diving into their journey to Baghdad and beyond. So, how about a little quiz on Chaldean history?"

"That's an excellent idea," said Mr. Yatooma, at once.

"I thought you'd appreciate that," I said.

"I like that as well," said Helen.

"I'm glad you do." I then turned to the children. "Can someone share the history of the Chaldeans in a nutshell?"

"Will that be walnuts, peanuts, or coconut?" asked John.

"John!" his mother scolded.

"That's pretty clever, John," I said, teasingly.

"The Chaldean history traces back thousands of years to southern Mesopotamia, to Prophet Abraham who was from Ur of the Chaldeans, and places like Ur, Nippur, and Babylon," said Mary, reading from her notes. She flipped the page. "They were part of Mesopotamia, the cradle of civilization."

I noticed everyone's eyes light up as she spoke, impressed.

"That's excellent, Mary," I said. "See children how notes can be helpful?"

"I took notes too, but on my iPhone," a kid in the back said.

"Oh, and what did your notes say?"

"The Chaldeans ruled Babylon during its golden age under King Nebuchadnezzar II," he said, stumbling a bit as he pronounced the name. "He built the Hanging Gardens, one of the Seven Wonders of the Ancient World, and brought the Jewish people to Babylon after taking over Jerusalem. They've found over a hundred clay tablets that show they lived decent lives there, with jobs, homes, and active communities."

"They were really spiritual and super scholarly," someone said, not even bothering to look at their notes.

"What an intelligent class," I said, turning to Mr. Yatooma. "You've done a great job as their teacher."

"Well, I give them some credit too," he replied with a wink to his students.

"Ha ha," one of them said. "Yeah, right."

"He's just trying to take all the credit."

"Classic Mr. Yatooma move."

I grinned and walked the group over to a softly glowing map of Mesopotamia. Arrows on the map showed the migration of the Chaldeans from southern Mesopotamia to northern Iraq and then eventually to Baghdad.

"In 1404, Giovanni, an Italian Dominican friar and Archbishop of the Sultanate, wrote about the Chaldeans as one of the main groups in Baghdad," I explained. "He wrote about them alongside Arabs, Syrians, Nestorians, Armenians, and Catholics. Giovanni even sent Dominican missionaries to minister to the Catholic Chaldeans. His writings describe Chaldea's plains, its people, and how invasions and religious changes shaped their journey over the centuries."

Mr. Yatooma slid a hand into his pocket. "You know, I don't think we mentioned Riccoldo da Monte Croce in the other galleries, did we?"

"Who's that?" Zaya asked, stroking an imaginary beard with exaggerated seriousness. "Sounds Italian, not Chaldean."

"Bingo!" Mr. Yatooma said, pulling his hand

out of his pocket and snapping his fingers. "He was Italian—a Dominican friar, kind of like Giovanni, but older and with way more miles on his sandals. This guy lived between 1243 and 1320, and let me tell you, he was quite the adventurer."

"An adventurer?" Lola asked, twirling her hair. "Like Indiana Jones?"

"Minus the hat and whip, but yeah, close enough," Mr. Yatooma said. "Around 1288, Riccoldo packed his bags, said goodbye to Italy, and headed east. He spent about a decade hanging out with all kinds of groups, including the Nestorians. And get this—he learned Arabic and Chaldean."

"Wait, an Italian guy who spoke Chaldean?" Zaya interrupted, eyebrows raised. "Seriously?"

"Seriously!" Mr. Yatooma said, throwing his hands up—and nearly knocking over one of the ancient books on display. "Oops! Almost turned history into a disaster. Anyway, in his book *Liber peregrinationis*—that's Latin for *Book of Travels*, by the way—Riccoldo wrote, 'These eastern Nestorians are all Chaldeans, and they pray and read in Chaldean.'"

"Who are the Nestorians?" someone asked.

"That's a huge topic," I said, tapping the face of my watch like I was checking if it still worked. "It would take a whole day to cover."

"Oh, please let's not do that!" Helen said.

"I know how to say the Lord's Prayer in Chaldean!" Mary said suddenly, looking up from her notebook with excitement.

"One of my favorite nuns teaches it online," another kid chimed in eagerly. "Want me to show you on my phone?"

"Oh, I know her!" Mary said. "She also teaches the Hail Mary!"

The kids started buzzing, their voices overlapping as they swapped stories about online lessons and prayers.

"Okay, okay!" I said, clapping my hands to calm them down. "I love that you're learning prayers in Chaldean. It's amazing! But save those videos for lunch break, okay?"

"When's lunch, anyway?" one of the kids groaned. "Feels like we've been here forever."

"Yeah, my mom packed some *tekhratha* I'm dying to eat," another jumped in.

"My mom sent *dolma*!" someone else bragged, sparking a playful debate about whose food was better.

"All this talk about food is making me hungry," Helen said.

"Me too," Mr. Yatooma said.

"Me three," I said with a chuckle. "But first, we need to finish this tour." I clapped my hands again, louder this time. "Alright, listen up! Let's focus for a bit, and I'll tell you how and why the Chaldeans ended up in Baghdad."

The chatter died down as the kids turned their attention back to me.

"Historically," I began, "Chaldeans lived in villages near Mosul in northern Iraq. These villages were their homes for centuries. But in the twentieth century, many Chaldeans started moving south to Baghdad for better jobs, education, and a safer, more modern life."

"I thought it was the other way around," Helen said. "Didn't they move to the villages to stay safe because they were isolated?"

"Great question," I said. "And you're right—they did move to isolated villages, but that was earlier, when they were looking for refuge from persecution. Those villages became strongholds of Chaldean culture and faith."

Some in the group nodded.

"But later," I continued, "as Iraq modernized, village life wasn't as practical. Farming didn't pay much, and there weren't many schools or job opportunities. Baghdad, on the other hand, offered all of that. Plus, the Chaldean Church moved its patriarchate—their spiritual headquarters—to Baghdad from Mosul in the mid-twentieth century, which made the city even more important for the community."

"So, they moved to the city for jobs and education?" Mary asked, scribbling furiously in her notebook.

"Yes," I said. "But also because of conflict. Wars and violence often destroyed villages or made them unsafe. Extremist groups targeted Chaldean communities, forcing many to leave. Some found refuge in Baghdad, while others fled Iraq altogether."

"It's a complicated story," Mr. Yatooma said, gesturing animatedly. "Both moves—to the villages and from the villages—are part of the Chaldean journey. You could say they were always adapting, finding ways to survive and thrive no matter where they went."

"This must've been so hard on them," Mary said, her pencil pausing mid-note.

"It was," I said. "But Chaldeans are resilient. In Baghdad, they built churches, schools, and businesses. They became merchants, doctors, teachers, and writers. They didn't just survive—they thrived and helped shape Baghdad into a center of culture and intellect."

"Tub?" John asked, frowning. "Like... a bathtub?"

"Hub," I said, biting back a laugh. "Like a center."

"Ohhh," John replied, wide-eyed, before covering his mouth. "Oops!"

The group burst into laughter, the sound echoing through the gallery as we moved toward a display of artifacts: trade ledgers, medical tools, and painted ceramic plates.

"These show the Chaldeans' contributions to Baghdad's markets," I explained. "They traded spices, fabrics, and ceramics, connecting Baghdad to faraway places like India and China. Chaldean doctors were also renowned, studying at institutions like Al-Mustansiriya, one of the world's oldest universities, founded in Baghdad in 1227."

"That's amazing," Mary said, her voice full of awe.

"It really is," I said. "Chaldeans played a vital role in Baghdad's legacy as a center of learning and culture."

Next, we approached a section dedicated to Al-Mutanabbi Street, Baghdad's historic book market. Shelves of books lined the walls, and the faint smell of old paper filled the air.

"This is Al-Mutanabbi Street," I said. "Remember, I mentioned him earlier in the exhibit? He's one of Baghdad's most famous poets, and this street was named after him. It's been a hub—not a tub—for literature for centuries." I shot a playful look at John, who immediately turned red but couldn't hold back a grin.

"Good one," he said, laughing.

"Chaldeans were part of this tradition," I continued, "writing and publishing books in Arabic, Chaldean, and other languages. Poetry was especially important to them, expressing their faith, struggles, and love for their homeland."

As I spoke, the air seemed to shimmer above the bookshelves. Suddenly, a glowing quill appeared, tracing a Chaldean poem in the air. The group gasped, leaning closer as the English translation glowed softly below:

Through the streets of Baghdad we wandered,
Our voices carried on the wind.
In the markets, in the churches,
Our stories found their home.

"This," I said quietly, "is what the Chaldeans brought to Baghdad—their voices, their stories, their resilience. It's what we're here to honor today."

The group stood in silence, captivated by the glowing words. Then Zaya broke it. "So… if this quill is magic, can we use it to write our homework faster?"

The group exchanged amused glances and a few grins, some shaking their heads at Zaya's comment.

"Nice try, Zaya," I said. "But I think you'll have to stick to pencils for that."

"Aw, worth a shot," Zaya said with a shrug.

"Next," I continued, "we explore the churches of Baghdad and the stories they hold. Ready for another adventure?"

"Ready!" the group chorused, their excitement renewed.

With that, we stepped toward the next section, the whispers of Chaldean history guiding us like a story still unfolding.

CHAPTER 3

Churches Through Time

The next gallery glowed with soft, golden light, casting warmth over intricate carvings and paintings of Baghdad's historic churches. The air carried the faint scent of frankincense, and the soft chime of bells echoed in the background. The children fell silent, their steps slowing, as if the room itself commanded reverence.

"This gallery celebrates the churches of Baghdad," I began. "They're not just buildings—they're the heartbeats of their neighborhoods, keepers of tradition, and witnesses to centuries of history."

"How many churches are there in Baghdad?" Zaya asked, bouncing slightly on his heels.

"Good question," I said, letting the moment linger. "There's one Roman Rite church, one Armenian church, four Syriac ones, and…" I paused for effect, "…nine Chaldean churches."

"Nine?!" John blurted as he hopped with excitement. "That's, like, a lot of praying!"

"It is," I said. "And each one holds a story waiting to be uncovered."

The group moved toward the room's centerpiece: a towering replica of St. Joseph's. The stained-glass windows radiated soft light, and the golden cross at its peak glimmered like a beacon.

"That's St. Joseph's!" Mary said, flipping open her notebook with a triumphant smile.

"Looks like you've done your homework," I said, "but I'll bet there's something here even you haven't discovered."

The children gathered closer and grew so quiet, you'd think you were in a library.

"There are two St. Joseph churches in Baghdad," I said.

"What?" Zaya's face scrunched in disbelief. "Two? Isn't one enough? Did they run out of names or something?"

"Apparently not," I said. "But they're not exactly the same. One is Chaldean, and the other is Latin. Both are Catholic, but they serve different communities."

"Are they like rival churches?" Zaya asked. "Do they have bake-offs or something?"

"Baklava vs. baklava!" John declared, framing his hands like a TV director.

The kids burst into laughter as Mr. Yatooma

shook his head. "Oh, I can see it now—a head-to-head cook-off. '*And the winner of Baghdad's Best Knafeh is…*'" He mimed tearing open an envelope with exaggerated drama.

The laughter rippled through the room as Lola inched toward a display case nearby. Her gaze fixed on a delicate rosary hanging from a hook. She reached out, brushing it with her fingers before I could intervene.

"Careful, Lola," I said gently. "No touching."

"Oh, sorry!" she squeaked, pulling back her hand and clasping it behind her back.

"Alright," I continued, signaling to a photo of the Latin St. Joseph. "The Latin church was built way back in 1871 for Baghdad's Roman Catholic community. Its thick brick walls keep it cool in the summer, warm in the winter, and its arched windows are inspired by the Abbasid era."

"It looks like it's sinking," Zaya said, squinting at the image.

"Well," I said, "technically, the ground around it has risen over time, but yeah, it's a little… low profile."

The kids giggled as I went on. "During World War I, it served as a hospital. By World War II, Polish troops were attending Mass there. But these days, it's in rough shape—neglect, fewer locals in the neighborhood, and the nearby busy Shorja Market don't help."

"What about the Chaldean Cathedral?" Mary asked, turning her attention to the replica.

"That's in better shape," I said, pointing to another display. "You know, Pope Francis celebrated Mass here in 2021."

"He did?" Mary said dreamily as Lola reached out toward the glowing cross atop the replica, her hand hovering inches away before I cleared my throat.

"Lola…"

She froze, grinning sheepishly. "I wasn't gonna touch it!"

Behind me, I heard a sharp thump. I turned just in time to see Zaya stumbling back, nearly knocking over a baptismal font.

"Whoa!" he yelped, steadying himself.

"Zaya," I said. "You're going to take out an entire sacrament if you're not careful!"

"Sorry," he said, holding his hands up defensively. "It startled me!"

"Alright, everyone, stay on your feet and keep your hands to yourselves," I said, tucking a strand of hair behind my ear as I turned back to the display. My fingers brushed the pendant of my necklace, a small pause to gather my thoughts. "Now, where were we? Oh yes—both churches tell different parts of Baghdad's story. The Latin one reflects the history of Western Catholics here, while the Chaldean one is a living symbol of Iraq's indigenous Christian community. Both are essential to understanding the city's rich heritage."

"Still," Zaya said, narrowing his eyes, "I'm not hanging out in a building that's halfway underground."

"Alright, Mr. Architect," Mr. Yatooma said, raising an eyebrow. "Let's not be so quick to judge. One's like a wise old storyteller, and the other's a modern symbol of strength. You need both to tell the full story."

The kids nodded thoughtfully, their chatter fading as they absorbed the weight of the history surrounding them.

I pointed to another display. "This is Our Lady of Sorrows. It's one of Baghdad's oldest churches, and the Chaldean community has worshiped here for over 180 years."

Mary leaned closer to the photograph. "It's smaller than the St. Joseph churches."

"It is," I said, "but it's just as important. The first church was built in 1843, but it kept flooding because it was so close to the Tigris River."

"So what did they do?" John asked.

"In 1889," I began, "they rebuilt it and raised the floor by about five meters to keep the water out."

"That's as high as a two-story building!" Mr. Yatooma said, raising his hand above his head to give the kids a clear sense of the height.

"And it took years to complete," I said. "The project finished in 1898. It's in a part of the Shorja district called Aqd al-Nasara—that means the 'Christian Quarter.'"

"Do people still go there?" John asked.

"They do," I said. "Even though fewer Christians live in the area now, it's still an active church. In 2015, Patriarch Louis Raphael I Sako led a big restoration project to preserve it."

The group was quiet again, their eyes lingering on the photograph.

Lola broke the silence. "Hey, isn't the St. Hirmiz Chaldean Church the one that was built around 430 AD in Baghdad?"

"Great memory, Lola, about the name and date," I said. "But it's actually in Turkey, in a region that, long ago, was considered part of Mesopotamia."

Mary tapped her pen against her cheek. "Turkey was part of Mesopotamia?"

Before I could answer, someone blurted out, "Why did they call it Turkey?"

"They like turkeys," Zaya said confidently, as if

it were the most obvious thing in the world. "Why else?"

A few kids snickered, and Mr. Yatooma stepped in before it spiraled further. Raising a hand to get their attention, he said, "Actually, the name comes from the Medieval Latin 'Turchia' or 'Turquia,' which means 'Land of the Turks.'"

But before the explanation could sink in, a few kids broke into exaggerated turkey gobbles. "Gobble-Gobble-Gobble!" one of the boys squawked, flapping his elbows like wings.

The noise grew louder as more kids joined in, cackling and stumbling over each other in laughter.

"Alright, enough, enough!" I said firmly, raising my voice above the chaos.

Mr. Yatooma tried to hide a smirk while Helen looked horrified.

"Let's move on to the next gallery," I said, waving them forward.

But they were already nearly running ahead, making garbled turkey sounds as they went. Mr. Yatooma and I exchanged a look, shaking our heads with a mix of amusement and exasperation. Along with Helen, we trailed behind the kids, their cackles echoing as they disappeared into the next exhibit.

CHAPTER 4

The Golden Threads of Trade

The cackling faded as the vibrant atmosphere of the next gallery captured the children's attention. Their laughter dissolved into quiet awe. The deep earth tones of the previous room gave way to hues of gold, crimson, and sapphire. The walls seemed alive with patterns resembling Persian carpets, and a faint, spicy aroma of saffron and incense floated in the air. Real carpets hung along the walls, their intricate designs glowing under the soft lighting.

"Children, you're allowed to feel the carpets," I said, eyeing Lola, who smiled at me and immediately reached out to touch one.

"It's so soft!" she said, running her hands over the colorful threads. A few kids followed her lead, marveling at the textures.

In the center of the room stood a large replica of a Baghdad bazaar, bustling with life. Stalls overflowed with silks, fragrant spices, glazed ceramics, and sparkling bolts of fabric.

"This gallery," I began, "is all about trade and commerce—one of the most important parts of Baghdad's history. The Chaldeans played a big role here as merchants and craftsmen, connecting Baghdad to the rest of the world."

Zaya's hand shot up. "Why was Baghdad such a big deal for trade?"

"It's all about location," I said, pointing to a glowing map on the wall. Golden lines stretched across it, connecting cities like Damascus, Constantinople, Samarkand, and even faraway China. "Baghdad was at the heart of the Silk Road—a network of trade routes that linked the East and West. Merchants from everywhere came here to buy and sell goods."

"Location, location, location!" a voice piped up from the back.

Everyone turned to see who had spoken.

"That's my uncle's motto," the boy said proudly. "He's a store owner."

The room erupted in laughter.

"What did they sell?" Mary asked, her pen darting across her notebook.

"Everything," I said. "Silks, spices, jewels, ceramics, books, ideas, and even …" I paused, letting the suspense build.

"Even what?" Zaya asked, his eyes wide.

"Liquor, arak, beer, and wine," I said, lowering my voice like I was sharing a secret.

John's jaw dropped. "Just like their liquor stores here?"

"That's right," I said. "Because they were Christians, they were allowed to sell alcohol—something Muslims couldn't do because of their religion. So, liquor became a big part of their business, and it gave them a unique role in the market."

Mr. Yatooma nodded. "It's true. For Muslims, drinking alcohol is forbidden in many Arab countries. The rules vary—some countries are stricter than others. In Iraq, for example, you might just get a fine."

"How harsh?" a voice asked.

"Maybe the death penalty," he said.

The kids gasped, then fell silent, absorbing the weight of what he'd said.

I broke the silence gently. "It wasn't an easy business to be in. Liquor store owners faced a lot of risks, especially when extremists started targeting their shops."

"She's right," Mr. Yatooma said. "In 2016, Iraq's parliament even passed a law banning the import, sale, and production of alcohol."

The mood in the room grew somber, the kids

shifting on their feet as they absorbed the weight of the discussion.

"What's arak?" a kid asked, his voice hesitant but intrigued.

The group turned toward him.

"Good question!" I said, adjusting my stance and clasping my hands. "Arak is a traditional Middle Eastern drink made from distilled grapes and flavored with anise. It's strong and has a licorice-like taste. People call it 'lion's milk' because it turns a cloudy, milky-white color when mixed with water—a process called louche."

"Lion's milk?" Zaya repeated. "I'll have some of that if it'll turn me into a lion!"

Mr. Yatooma scratched his head, giving a low chuckle. "Not sure you're ready for that strong flavor."

"Plus, you're nowhere near the proper age," Helen said, crossing her arms and adjusting her glasses as if to emphasize her point. She shot Mr. Yatooma a sharp look, as though that was the bigger issue.

"You've got a point, Helen," he said with a small nod. "But kids, remember Ninkasi?"

A few hands went up.

"The goddess of beer!" Lola said, her voice bright.

"That's right, Lola," he said, tapping the edge of a wooden barrier for emphasis. "Her priestesses brewed fresh beer every day and sang a hymn in her honor. Want to know why?"

The kids stood a little straighter, their attention locked on him.

"Most people didn't know how to read," he said, now resting a hand on the wood. "So, they memorized the beer recipe by singing it. Pretty clever, huh?"

"Women are so smart," Mary said with a deep, satisfied sigh.

"Absolutely!" he replied, nodding firmly. "And back then, beer was healthier than water. Everybody drank it—men, women, even kids like you!"

The group burst into giggles, and Zaya mimed chugging an imaginary mug of beer, swaying dramatically as if he were tipsy.

"Alright, alright," I said, clapping my hands to refocus the group. "Chaldeans—whether in their villages, cities like Baghdad, or new homes in the West—were known for opening mom-and-pop shops. Their merchants were highly respected for being honest, skilled, and resourceful. They knew that by working hard, providing good service, and selling what people needed, they could not only survive but thrive. It's a tradition they've carried wherever they've gone."

Helen, usually quick with a snarky remark,

surprised everyone by saying, "That's so nice. It's like they were always helping their communities and contributing to their home country."

"That's a beautiful way to put it," I said, then motioned toward the next room. "Now, let's head to the next exhibit: The Rise of Learning."

As the group began to shuffle forward, Lola lingered for a moment, her fingers brushing over one of the hanging carpets. A few other kids paused, following her lead, tracing the intricate patterns with quiet fascination before hurrying to catch up. The rich scent of saffron and spices hung in the air as we stepped toward the next chapter of Baghdad's remarkable story.

CHAPTER 5

The City of Learning

The next gallery hummed with quiet library vibes. Shelves lined the walls, filled with replicas of books, scrolls, and ancient manuscripts. The soft sound of pages turning echoed in the background, creating an atmosphere of discovery.

"This gallery," I said, gesturing to the displays, "is dedicated to a time when learning flourished across cultures and religions. Scholars from different backgrounds came to Baghdad to share and expand knowledge."

The group gathered around a display featuring a miniature replica of the House of Wisdom, a grand structure with arched doorways and a courtyard bustling with tiny scholar figurines.

"What's the House of Wisdom?" Zaya asked as he studied the model.

"It was like the world's greatest library and research center," I explained. "Founded in Baghdad during the Abbasid Caliphate, it became a hub where scholars from all over the world—Muslims, Christians, Jews, and others—came to study and translate vital work."

"Imagine walking through the halls of the House of Wisdom," Mr. Yatooma said. "Scholars debating under the arches, scribes translating ancient texts at their desks, and shelves overflowing with scrolls and manuscripts from all over the world."

"Sounds like an era of intellectual exchange," Helen said.

"I want to do a student exchange one day," said a girl who had never spoken before.

All eyes looked at her.

"That's a wonderful idea…" I began.

"What kind of stuff did they study?" Mary interrupted, jotting down notes.

"Everything," I said. "Astronomy, mathematics, medicine, philosophy, engineering, and more. Scholars translated ancient Chaldean, Hebrew, Latin, Greek, Persian, and Indian texts into Arabic, making knowledge accessible to more people than ever before."

"I would've loved to have been a scholar in those days," Mary said, hugging her notebook and staring far, far away.

"Your role as a scholar would've been priceless there," I said. "You know, in Babylon, Nebuchadnezzar had thousands of scribes. They recorded everything from temple rituals to grain inventories on clay tablets using cuneiform. They were essential—then and now. Without their work, much of what we know about ancient Mesopotamia would've been lost."

"Nebuchadnezzar would've hired you in a heartbeat, Mary," said Mr. Yatooma.

She blinked in awe, blushing.

"Could you hook me a job at Ishtar Gate?" Zaya asked.

"Oh, me too!" Lola said, her hand over her chest. "I'd love something in the Hanging Gardens where I just know aliens helped water the plants."

"I want in too," said John. "I can be the jokester."

This caused the children to chit-chat about the types of jobs they were fit for during the Chaldean Empire when someone asked, "Ms. Weam, is the House of Wisdom still open for the public?"

I paused, my tone becoming more somber. "The original House of Wisdom no longer exists. It was destroyed in 1258, during the Siege of Baghdad by the Mongol army."

The group looked up at me with tremendously disappointed expressions.

"Led by Hulagu Khan, the Mongols sacked the city," I said. "They destroyed all its contents—books, manuscripts, even any illustrations that might have existed. These precious treasures were thrown into the Tigris River. People said that the river turned blue from the ink of the books."

The children gasped.

"The destruction of the House of Wisdom marked the end of Baghdad's Golden Age," I continued softly. "But its legacy lives on. Over the centuries, artists have imagined what it might have looked like, and today, there's a modern library and cultural center in Sharjah, UAE, also called the House of Wisdom. It's a stunning building that celebrates learning in the same spirit as the original."

The group lingered for a moment, absorbing the weight of what had been lost. Yet, as they turned to the next display, a sense of curiosity began to replace their somber expressions.

"What's this?" Zaya asked, pointing to a black-and-white photo of students sitting attentively in a classroom, their notebooks open.

"This is Baghdad College," I said, stepping closer. "It was one of the most prestigious schools in Iraq, founded by Jesuit priests to provide a world-class education. Many Chaldeans attended this school, including my father, and it became an important part of their community."

"Your father attended this school?" Mary asked. "What did he study?"

"Well, he wanted to be a doctor but ended up mastering numbers," I said.

Mr. Yatooma, admiring a display of the school's peak years, turned to the group. "Ms. Weam's father was a genius. He was hired right away at Baghdad's Railway Station and became head of the accounting department."

I smiled, touched by his words. They brought back memories of my father's love for books and the quiet pride he took in his work.

Shaking off the thought, I turned to the group. "The Jesuits believed education could empower communities and bring people together. Baghdad College produced some of Iraq's brightest minds—doctors, engineers, writers, and leaders. Graduates were always in high demand."

"Who were the Jesuits?" Lola asked.

"They were priests from the New England Province in the United States," I explained. "They came to Baghdad at the request of Chaldean Patriarch Mar Emmanuel II Toma and founded Baghdad College in 1932. The school was for Christian boys, but students of all faiths—Muslims, Jews—were welcomed. They taught in both Arabic and English."

"Fun fact, kids," said Mr. Yatooma. "Baghdad College wasn't just about academics. It also had one of the best sports programs in the country. Their basketball and soccer teams were legendary!"

"Sports and science?" Zaya said, raising an eyebrow. "That's a cool combo."

"I love combos," said John, and groaned, "and can't wait for our lunch break."

The children laughed.

Before the topic of food sneaks back in, I led them to a display of cuneiform tablets. "These," I said, "are replicas of the Chaldean Astronomical Diaries."

"Diaries?" Mary asked, her ears perking up.

"Astronomical?" Lola asked, her voice full of inquisitiveness.

Both asked their questions at the same time, their excitement spilling over into laughter.

"Yes," I said. "The originals date back as far as 650 BC and were found in the library of the Assyrian King Ashurbanipal in Nineveh. Today, they're displayed in the British Museum."

"What are they?" Zaya asked, squeezing between the other kids to get a closer look.

"They're one of the longest-running scientific records in history," I explained. "The Chaldeans of southern Babylonia were the scientists of their time. These seventy tablets recorded centuries of astronomical observations. The Chaldeans believed the movements of the planets and stars were messages from the gods, but they didn't just guess what they meant—they studied the skies, collected data, and discovered patterns."

"Ancient scientists," Zaya said with pride.

"That, they were," I said. "And their methods of observation and data collection became the foundation of modern astronomy—and science itself. They even warned rulers when they believed celestial events predicted something important, like an eclipse or a bad omen."

"Wow," Mary whispered, staring at the tablets as if they were shinning stars.

The children stood in silence for a moment as they gazed at the cuneiform etched into stone.

Finally, Mary broke the quiet. "Does Baghdad College still exist?"

I sighed, my voice tinged with sadness. "Unfortunately, no. Baghdad College faced challenges during Iraq's political upheavals. The Jesuits who ran it were expelled when the Baathist government took over the school in 1969."

Mary's face fell. "That's so sad. I can't imagine losing my school."

"It wasn't just the loss of a school," Mr. Yatooma said. "It was the loss of a place where students from all backgrounds came together to learn, play, and dream about a brighter future."

"It was a sad chapter in history," I said. "But its legacy lives on in the students who studied there and the communities they went on to serve. It shaped generations of brilliant minds who carried its spirit of learning and unity into the world."

I let the words linger a bit before I spoke again, my voice filled with hope. "As the Book of Daniel says, 'Those who are wise will shine like the brightness of the heavens, and those who lead many to righteousness, like the stars for ever and ever.'"

The quote lifted the seriousness from the children's faces, like sunlight melting frost on a window.

I was glad for this shift of attitude and glanced at my phone to check the time.

"Now," I said, leading them forward, "let's explore Baghdad's neighbors—the different communities that have lived here side by side."

"Like a bee nest?" someone asked.

"Yes, like a bee nest," I said.

As the group followed, the children whispered amongst themselves. "Do you think they really predicted eclipses back then?" Zaya asked.

"I mean, they were super smart," Mary replied. "Like…scientists and historians rolled into one."

"And don't forget magicians," Lola said, "and maybe, possibly, quite likely extraterrestrials."

A few children snickered.

"Don't laugh," she said, defensively. "I think Hollywood got the idea of E.T. from Chaldeans."

The children roared with laughter, teasing Lola about her wild ideas. She stood her ground, confident. As their voices faded and we moved deeper into the gallery, those wild ideas began to feel, to me, maybe, possibly, quite likely, not so wild after all.

CHAPTER 6

The Neighbors of Baghdad

The children chitter-chattered into the next gallery.
One of them nearly tripped over the slightly elevated
threshold, almost causing a domino effect.

"Be careful," I warned, along with Helen and Mr.
Yatooma.

One pretended to fall over, another mimicked
her, and the adults demanded for everyone to "be-
have!" They quickly composed themselves, straightened their clothes, and soon started to marvel at their
surroundings. Murals stretched across the walls, capturing the city's vibrant neighborhoods: women bal-
ancing baskets of fruit in a bustling market, children
darting through narrow alleyways, and shopkeep-
ers leaning on counters piled high with spices. The
sounds of the city filled the air—the call to prayer
blending with distant church bells, the soft chants
of hymns, and the rhythmic splashing of water from
a Mandaean baptism. The children's awes and oohs
were music to my ears.

"Whoa," Zaya muttered. "This place is next level."

"Baghdad during the Abbasid era *was* next level," Mr. Yatooma said. "It was alive, electric! The New York City of its time, but with fewer yellow cabs."

Suddenly, Arabic beat pulsated through the gallery. The children started moving their bodies to the rhythm.

"For centuries, Muslims, Christians, Jews, Mandaeans, and others shared Baghdad's streets," I said, watching them have a good time. "They traded, debated, celebrated—and yes, sometimes clashed."

"You see, Baghdad wasn't some utopia where everyone held hands and sang kumbaya," Mr. Yatooma said. "Yes, they lived, worked, and worshipped in the same parts of the city, and yes, they often got along beautifully. But they didn't *always* get along."

"They didn't?" Mary asked.

"No, there were tensions," he said. "Non-Muslims, for example, had to pay a special tax called the *jizya* and they were, well, considered second class citizens."

"Meaning what?" Helen asked.

"Meaning they did not have the same rights as Muslims," I said.

"They couldn't, for instance, have certain jobs such as become a judge and definitely not a president of a company."

"How about the president of their country?" a boy standing on the side asked. "Could they do that?"

"How could they run a country if they can't even run a company?" Zaya asked, throwing up his hands like it was the most obvious thing in the world.

"Those are two different things," the boy defended himself and an argument ensued, followed by some of the boys starting to shove each other.

"Listen up!" Mr. Yatooma jumped in and gave them a look they could not ignore. They stopped in their tracks. Then he turned to me. "Go ahead, Ms. Weam, the floor is all yours."

I tugged at my sleeves and began as if nothing had happened. "Now, despite the differences that sometimes caused friction, there were long periods of coexistence and intellectual collaboration between these communities."

"Hallelujah," someone said, giggling.

We moved to a display featuring artifacts from Baghdad's Jewish community: Torah scrolls, menorahs, and a beautifully illustrated Haggadah.

"The Jews of Baghdad," I said, "were one of the city's oldest communities, dating back to the Babylonian exile in the sixth century BCE. During the Abbasid era, they played an integral role in Baghdad's society."

"What did they do?" Lola asked, observing the menorahs.

"Many were merchants, scholars, and doctors," I said. "Some of the most famous Jewish thinkers, like Saadia Gaon, lived here. They contributed to philosophy, science, and medicine—and shared ideas with their Muslim and Christian neighbors. Jewish scholars even collaborated with others at the House of Wisdom, translating and preserving ancient texts."

"Were they treated fairly?" Mary asked, her pen up in the air.

"Well," I said, "it depended on the time and the ruler. Under Islamic law, Jews like Christians had the status of *dhimmis*, or protected people, which allowed them to practice their religion but that also came with restrictions. Aside from the tax they had to pay, they couldn't testify against Muslims in certain cases, and they were sometimes required to wear distinctive clothing."

I paused, then elaborated, "But the Abbasid rulers often valued knowledge and expertise above all else. During times of stability, Jewish scholars, merchants, and financiers thrived and contributed greatly to Baghdad's intellectual and economic life. Unfortunately, during periods of political instability, tensions flared, and minority communities, including the Jews, oftentimes became scapegoats."

Helen straightened her glasses. "Is there a Jewish community left in Baghdad?"

I hesitated, searching for the right words. "Not really. At its peak in the 1940s, there were over 150,000 Jews in Iraq. Today, there are fewer than four left in the entire country, according to a number of reports."

The group fell silent, reality settling over them like a shadow.

"That's heartbreaking," Helen said, her hands dropping over her polka dot dress.

"It is," I agreed. "But it's also a reminder of how precious history is—and why we have to preserve it, even when the communities themselves are nearly gone."

As we moved to a section highlighting Baghdad's Muslim majority, I turned to the group. "You know, my siblings and I were all born in Baghdad. We had Muslim friends, neighbors, classmates… In fact, my best friend growing up was a Muslim girl named Niran. Her mom treated me like her own. I'll never forget their kindness. We loved each other very much."

The group was quiet for a moment, absorbing the personal connection.

"Same with my family," Mr. Yatooma said. "Our homes were among Muslims and today, I'm still in contact with my college friends who are Muslim. Baghdad wasn't perfect, but there's a saying: people with good hearts always find each other."

"Baghdad's story teaches us that coexistence is possible," said Mr. Yatooma, "but it requires effort, empathy, and understanding."

"Like here in America," Helen said, her finger on her chin as if the thought had just occurred to her.

"Yes, thank you for that," I said. "We weren't able to co-exist in Iraq, but here, we are."

I led the group down the corridor until we reached a statue of Kahramana in a glowing display. Her elegant figure stood poised, pouring oil into jars where the forty thieves hid."

"This is Kahramana," I explained, "from the story of *Ali Baba and the Forty Thieves*. She was a clever servant who saved her master by outsmarting the thieves."

"Why is she so important?" Helen asked.

"Well, for one," I said, "she's a reminder of the power of quick thinking and courage. But more than that, Kahramana represents how storytelling can bring people together. The tale of Ali Baba is part of *One Thousand and One Nights*, a collection of stories that came from all over—Arabic, Persian, Indian, and Mesopotamian cultures. It wasn't written by one person or even one religion. Instead, it reflects how stories can transcend borders, religions, and nationalities to connect us all."

Mr. Yatooma nodded thoughtfully. "Stories like this remind us of our shared humanity. No matter where we come from, we all love tales of bravery, cleverness, and hope."

"This statue was created by the renowned Iraqi sculptor Mohammed Ghani Hikmat in 1971," I added as the group stood admiring the statue. "It's now one of Baghdad's most beloved landmarks."

"Is that cooking oil or olive oil?" Zaya broke the silence, eyeing the vase.

"I'll taste it and find out," John said, reaching for the jar Kahramana held.

Helen grabbed his hand and spun him around like a wind-up toy. "Let's go this way, Wise Guy," she said, marching him off.

Naturally, we all followed—some of us more out of curiosity than loyalty. As we walked away from the statue, I couldn't help but think about how stories like Kahramana's keep history alive, even when the people are no longer here.

CHAPTER 7

Festivals of the Tigris

The next gallery was a feast for the senses. Bright banners swayed from the ceiling, embroidered with Chaldean crosses, crescent moons, Stars of David, and Mandaean symbols. The air was alive with the sounds of laughter, music, and the faint rhythm of drums, as if we'd stepped into a festival. Tables were set with replica foods, and mannequins dressed in festive clothing were posed mid-dance or mid-laugh, capturing the joy of celebration.

Mary and Lola took it upon themselves to mimic the mannequins' poses, while Zaya and John played photographers, shouting things like, "Work it! Own the moment!" Other kids pretended to sample the food, offering exaggerated reviews like, "Mmm, divine!" or "Ugh, this fake hummus is *so* last century." Watching them interact with the displays was like watching a slapstick comedy unfold in a museum.

"Whose flag is that?" Helen asked, pointing at the striking flag hung near the entrance.

"That's the Chaldean flag," I said.

"Oh," she said, seeming surprised. "I didn't know there's a Chaldean flag."

"Yes, there is," I said, stepping closer to the design of vibrant blue lines and golden star. "It was designed by Dr. Amer Hanna Fatuhi in 1985. He's a historian, writer, and artist who wanted to create a modern symbol that honors Chaldean heritage. You see those two blue lines? They represent the Tigris and Euphrates rivers. The yellow circle is the sun, the blue circle is the moon, and the eight-pointed star in the center is inspired by ancient Babylonian symbols."

"So, he basically gave us an astronomy lesson on a flag?" Zaya asked, squinting at the star.

"He did," I said. "It ties back to Chaldean contributions to astronomy, math, law, and justice. It's a modern flag, but its design reflects thousands of years of Mesopotamian history. It's a fitting place for it since this gallery is all about the festivals of Baghdad and the surrounding areas."

We moved to a mural of families picnicking by the Tigris.

"For centuries," I continued, "Chaldeans and their neighbors—Muslims, Jews, Mandaeans, Zoroastrians—celebrated life, faith, and community along the Tigris River."

Zaya glanced at the mural and muttered, "Too bad we can't taste the food for real."

"True," I said, "but at least you won't have to pretend to like it."

I gestured toward the scene. "Springtime was magical by the river. For the Chaldeans, it marked Akitu, the ancient Babylonian New Year festival, which celebrated renewal and the planting season."

"What did they do for Akitu?" Mary asked, Mary asked, her pen flying across her notebook.

"Originally, it was a pagan festival, but the Chaldeans adapted it," I explained. "Families shared meals, wore floral garlands, and performed group dances to honor their ancestors and pray for a good harvest. It was a time of hope and joy."

"What does that design represent?" Lola asked, pointing at a Persian banner.

"Nowruz, the Persian New Year," I said. "It has been around for over 3,000 years. It's celebrated by Zoroastrians, many Muslims, and even some Chaldeans. People clean their homes, visit family, and embrace a fresh start. In Baghdad, it's a tradition that unites everyone—though some may just show up for the food!"

Some of the children giggled.

"Look at the boat rides!" Zaya said, gesturing toward a mural of people on the Tigris.

"Beautiful, isn't it?" I asked. "Families would picnic by the river, release lanterns, and even race boats. Sometimes, though, these celebrations became tragic. Like in 2019, when a ferry capsized in Mosul during Nowruz, and many people, including children, lost their lives."

The group fell silent for a moment before I led them to the next section about religious festivals. A table was set with traditional foods: roasted lamb, dates, pastries, and more.

"For the Chaldeans, Easter was one of the biggest celebrations," I said, showing them a basket of painted brown eggs and a miniature nativity scene. "After Lent, families would come together for a feast, dye eggs in onion skins, and share dishes like pacha— boiled cow or sheep heads, legs, and stomachs."

"Oooh, I love pacha—except the tongue and eyes," a kid chimed in.

"Tongue?" Zaya asked, sticking his tongue out. "My mom doesn't use that, just skulls."

"Skulls?" Mary gasped, dropping her pen like it had suddenly caught fire.

Helen looked pale. "Oh, no. I think I'm going to faint."

"Alright, let's move on to desserts!" I said quickly, worried Helen might leave a very different kind of mark on the museum floor. "They made kleicha—sweet pastries filled with dates or nuts."

"Phew," Mary said, exhaling dramatically. "Much better."

"Why were their Easter eggs only brown?" a kid asked.

"Well," I said, "they didn't have the kind of food coloring we use today. Instead, they'd boil onion skins, which turned the water brown, and dip the eggs in that."

"That's interesting," Helen said, looking slightly less queasy.

"What about the other groups?" John asked.

"Muslims celebrated Ramadan and Eid al-Fitr," I explained. "During Ramadan, they fasted all day and broke their fast at night with dates, soup, and sweets. Eid was all about feasting and family. Jewish families had Passover, Rosh Hashanah, and Purim, with foods like matzo and honey cakes. And the Mandaeans celebrated Parwanaya—a five-day festival with baptisms and shared meals."

"And they all celebrated by the river?" Helen asked.

"Not exactly," I said, guiding them toward the mural. "Festivals along the Tigris changed throughout history. They evolved with the diverse peoples who lived here—from Sumerian and Babylonian rites to Mandaean baptisms and Ramadan feasts. But regardless of the times, the river was always a gathering place, connecting everyone to its life-giving waters."

As we explored, the air shimmered, and the mural seemed to come alive. Boats drifted on the glowing river, families laughed under starry skies, and dancers spun in circles, their robes flowing like waves. Everyone watched in silence, captivated by the scene.

"So, what's the takeaway here?" Mr. Yatooma asked, breaking the spell.

"That celebrations bring people together," Mary said.

"And that food is super important," Zaya added with a grin.

"And that this is the coolest museum ever!" Lola said, bouncing with excitement.

"Thank you, Lola," I said, touched by her words. "Now, let's head to the next section: the famous Chaldeans of Baghdad."

"Oh, this is going to be my favorite part!" Mary said, clapping her hands.

"Mine too," I said, giving her shoulder a gentle touch as we moved on.

CHAPTER 8

Assimilation and Identity

The next gallery was quieter, more contemplative than the others. The soft hum of conversation in Arabic and Aramaic floated through the air, occasionally mingling with the imagined sound of church bells and the adhan, the Islamic call to prayer.

"This gallery," I began, "is about assimilation—how Chaldeans became an integral part of Iraqi culture while still preserving their identity. For centuries, they adapted to life in Baghdad and beyond, adopting the language, customs, and traditions of their neighbors while holding on tightly to their own heritage..."

I trailed off as I noticed two students yawning, one rubbing his eyes, and another—impressively—standing up asleep, swaying like a palm tree in a storm.

"Ah, I see this topic is captivating to some of you," I said dryly.

Before I could go further, Mr. Yatooma stepped forward with the energy of a game show host. "Ms.

Weam, let me take the wheel for a second," he said, clasping his hands together. "I think I can wake up our sleepy adventurers here."

He marched over to a massive photograph of Baghdad's iconic Freedom Monument, which loomed over Tahrir Square in all its glory. The group perked up slightly.

"This," he bellowed, his voice reverberating like he was addressing a stadium, "is the *Nasb al-Hurri-yah*, the Freedom Monument. Designed by the one, the only, Jawad Saleem, the Leonardo da Vinci of Iraq! Finished in 1961, after the overthrow of the Hashemite monarchy, this masterpiece is more than just a pretty thing to look at. It's a story. A journey. A whole vibe. And guess what? You're about to hear all about it."

Lola squinted at the figures. "What are those people doing up there?"

"Oh, I'm so glad you asked," Mr. Yatooma said, rubbing his hands together like he was about to reveal a magic trick. "Let's break it down, shall we?" He pointed to the first figure.

"See that bolting horse there? That's the spark of revolution—the moment resistance begins, wild and fearless. Surrounding it, you've got four men, symbolizing the unity of people standing up and saying, 'Enough is enough!'"

He moved on to the next figure, his voice dropping dramatically. "And here… we have the suffering woman. She represents all the hardship endured before the revolution. She's not just sad—she's every tear ever cried, every hardship ever endured."

The kids leaned in, intrigued.

"Now this one," he said, pointing, "is martyrdom and grief. A martyr surrounded by three weeping women—a mother, a sister, and a wife. This is sacrifice, folks. This is the price of freedom."

"Wait," Zaya interrupted. "What's that guy in the cage?"

"Ah, excellent question!" Mr. Yatooma said, snapping his fingers. "That's the prisoner of thought. He's behind bars, but his ideas? Oh, they're not staying locked up. They're spreading, baby. They're spreading like wildfire!"

He moved to the next figure, his voice booming. "And here comes the cavalry!"

"Cavalry?" John asked, frowning. "Is that the same as caviar?"

"Isn't caviar *beta*?" Zaya chimed in, using the Chaldean word for eggs.

"It's fish, not eggs," Lola said confidently.

"Actually, it's fish eggs," Mary corrected, rolling her eyes.

"Cavalry—help, support," Mr. Yatooma explained.

"The revolutionary soldier! Breaking prison bars like he's in an action movie, liberating the people and paving the way for freedom."

"What about the torch lady?" asked Mary.

"That," Mr. Yatooma said, his tone reverent, "is freedom and enlightenment. She's like Iraq's own Statue of Liberty, carrying a torch to light the way. She says, 'Come on, folks, we've got work to do!'"

The kids giggled as he mimicked her pose, holding an imaginary torch.

"And here's the finale," he said, pointing to the last set of figures. "Peace and prosperity. Doves on the shoulders of a calm woman—because nothing says peace like some happy birds. And those two women? They represent the Tigris and Euphrates, Iraq's lifeblood, its rivers, its wealth. Oh, and don't forget the bull! That's a Mesopotamian symbol of fertility, reminding everyone of Iraq's ancient heritage."

"What about this guy with the hammer?" Zaya asked.

"He represents industry," Mr. Yatooma explained. "And those two farmers with the shovel? One represents an Arab, the other a Kurd. Together, they symbolize the national unity of Iraqis, working side by side to build the future."

The group stared at the image, their earlier boredom replaced with awe and excitement.

"Thank you for that dramatic performance," I said, truly impressed.

"You're welcome," he said with a playful bow. "I'm here all day."

As we moved on, I noticed how much more alive the children seemed, and I wondered if the museum would ever hire Mr. Yatooma as a docent—when he wasn't teaching, of course. With his knack for story-telling, he'd probably double attendance in no time.

We moved toward a display of manuscripts written in both Syriac and Arabic.

"Language is one of the clearest examples of assimilation," I said. "Our native tongue, Chaldean, is an ancient dialect of Aramaic—the language Jesus spoke. But as Chaldeans lived and worked alongside their Muslim, Jewish, and Mandaean neighbors, they also learned Arabic."

"Why Arabic?" Mary asked, jotting in her notebook.

"Arabic was the language of the Abbasid Caliphate," I explained. "It was the language of government, trade, and scholarship. If you wanted to thrive in Baghdad, you had to speak it. Over time, Arabic became the primary language for most Chaldeans in the cities."

"But they didn't forget Chaldean, right?" Zaya asked, his brow furrowed.

"Not at all," I said. "Chaldean stayed alive in the

church, especially during religious rituals. And over the years, other languages were incorporated too—like English, for instance."

The group moved to a section that recreated a typical Chaldean home in Baghdad. A woven rug covered the floor, a brass coffee pot gleamed on a low table, and a radio softly played Arabic music in the background.

"Chaldeans lived much like their neighbors," I said. "They wore similar clothes, ate similar foods, and celebrated many of the same holidays. They were part of the fabric of Iraqi society."

"Did women wear the hijab?" Lola asked.

"No, they didn't, but many wore an abaya, which was used mostly for convenience," I said. "My mom, for instance, wore it over her house clothes when she was heading to the market. The purpose was not to cover their hair, just so they don't have to change."

"What kind of food did they eat?" Lola asked.

"Delicious food," I said. "Chaldeans had their own special recipes, like *hareesa*, a porridge made from wheat and chicken, often served during religious holidays. But they also adopted many Iraqi dishes—*dolma* (stuffed grape leaves), *kubba* (fried dumplings filled with meat), and *masgouf* (grilled fish)."

"Where did dolma even come from?" Zaya asked, his curiosity piqued.

"Oh, everyone wants to claim that one!" I said with a grin. "The Turks say it's theirs—the word dolma is Turkish, meaning 'stuffed.' But ancient Persia had its own version, and the Greeks were stuffing leaves way back in the day, too. It's the ultimate shared dish."

Mr. Yatooma chimed in, "Kubba is just as global. The word comes from Aramaic, but you'll find different versions in Syria, Jordan, and even Brazil! Food doesn't care about borders—it just travels and adapts, just like people do."

"And masgouf," I added, "is pure Iraq. It's been grilled over open flames on the banks of the Tigris since ancient Mesopotamian times. It's more than a meal—it's a tradition."

"I'm seriously getting hangry," John said, rubbing his stomach.

"Me too," someone else mumbled as the kids began to grumble about lunch.

"We're almost there," I said, realizing I must speed up the tour a bit.

"How almost is almost?" someone else asked.

"Well, this wedding mural is *almost* the end of this exhibit," I said. "Weddings are a perfect example of how Chaldeans blended traditions with Iraqi culture. A Chaldean wedding might start with a traditional church ceremony, but the celebration afterward would often feature Arabic music, dancing, and plenty of food. At my wedding, we had a Chaldean band that sang in both Arabic and Chaldean, a DJ playing American songs, and, yes, even a belly dancer."

"I remember that," Mr. Yatooma said with a wink.

I brushed past his comment quickly. "Assimilation can be a magical thing."

The mural shifted to another scene, showing a family gathered around a table laden with food. "During Christmas and Easter, Chaldeans often invited neighbors to share meals, blending traditions regardless of faith," I said.

Nearby, photographs highlighted Chaldeans as teachers, doctors, merchants, and artists. "By the twentieth century, Chaldeans were deeply integrated into Iraqi society," I explained. "They were known for their education and craftsmanship and became leaders in fields like medicine, politics, and business."

"Was assimilation a natural part of their journey, or did they face challenges?" Helen asked.

"Of course, they faced challenges," I said. "There were times they faced discrimination or pressure to assimilate completely. For instance, in an attempt to Arabize the land, Chaldeans had to let go of their family last name and replace it with first name, middle name, which was the father's name, and last name, the grandfather's name."

"Why did they do that?" Lola asked. "It doesn't make sense."

"It was an attempt to disconnect people from their original ancestors," I said. "They figured that over time, people would forget their heritage. But our people always found ways to adapt while staying true to their roots."

The final display featured a church altar with candles, a cross, and a Syriac Bible.

"Faith was key to preserving their identity," I said. "The church wasn't just a place of worship. It was where Chaldeans spoke and sang hymns in their native tongue and passed down their heritage to the next generation."

The group stood quietly for a moment, reflecting.

"This," I said softly, "is the story of assimilation—finding a balance between embracing the culture of your home and honoring the traditions of your ancestors."

CHAPTER 9

Famous Chaldeans of Baghdad

In the next gallery, portraits adorned the walls, showing Chaldeans who had left their mark on Baghdad
and beyond. A timeline ran along the base of the
walls, highlighting their achievements in journalism, politics, and art.

"This gallery," I began, "is dedicated to the
Chaldeans who made history. They were pioneers,
leaders, and visionaries who broke barriers and inspired generations." I gestured to a large portrait of a
confident older woman with glasses. "This is Mariam
Nerma," I said. "She was the first woman journalist
in Iraq, and she was Chaldean."

"The first ever?" Mary asked, touching her jour-
nal as if it were a diamond.

"Yes," I said. "She was born on April 3, 1890, with
family roots in Tel Keppe. Her groundbreaking career began in 1921, just after World War I and before Iraq became a modern state. She wrote for *Dar
Al-Salam* newspaper, and her very first article made

history as the first-ever article written by a woman in Iraq."

"Tell us more, please!" Mary said urgently, her tone abandoning its usual calmness.

"Well," I said, "Mariam grew up in a world where women's lives were very limited. Almost no women could read, and opportunities for education were almost nonexistent, especially under the Ottoman rule. But her parents broke the norm and enrolled her in school. After excelling in her studies and even going to secondary school—unheard of for girls in Baghdad at the time—she returned to Baghdad determined to make a difference."

"What a cool girl," Zaya said. "What did she write about?"

"She had a vision," I said. "Mariam used her platform to advocate for women's rights, including access to education, laws against gender-based violence, and the right for women to enter the workforce. She was fearless in criticizing societal norms and even debated controversial topics publicly. Her influence was so significant that local newspapers began dedicating columns to women's issues because of her."

"Wow," Helen said with utmost excitement, forgetting herself. "She sounds amazing."

"She was," I agreed. "She didn't stop at writing articles. In 1937, Mariam founded *The Arab Girl*

Newspaper, the first high-quality newspaper in Iraq managed entirely by women—from writing to editing to distribution. It was a bold move, especially since running a newspaper was financially risky. She even used her own house as the headquarters and hung a wooden sign above it with the paper's name."

"Did it work?" Lola asked.

"It did, for a while," I said. "But Mariam refused to compromise her values. When the British Embassy offered to fund the newspaper in exchange for publishing pro-British propaganda, she refused, saying, 'I will not be a traitor to Iraq.' Unfortunately, financial struggles forced her to shut it down after just nine months."

"What happened after that?" Zaya asked.

"Mariam continued to write for prominent newspapers," I said. "She also worked as a teacher, inspiring young girls to pursue education, independence, and ambition. Her legacy as a feminist icon and pioneer in Iraqi journalism paved the way for future generations."

"What was her writing like?" Mary asked as she stared at her own writing.

"She was bold," I said. "Her articles were direct and powerful. She didn't just promote women's rights—she also criticized women who, in her words, were 'lost, submissive, and without ambition.' She believed education was women's most powerful weapon and made that the center of her message."

The children, especially the girls, looked at me with awe.

"Of course, further back, we have Elias al-Musili, a Chaldean priest who was the first Middle Easterner to travel to the Americas, a journey which occurred between 1668 and 1683," I said. "He was originally from Baghdad, although his name implies his family came from Mosul."

"Wasn't Maria born in Baghdad too?" John asked.

"No, dummy, weren't you listening this whole time?" someone said, and we all shot that kid a look.

"Now, now, no calling names," I said.

"But come on, we've talked about Maria a million times," Zaya said. "He should know it by heart."

"We have not gone through it a million times," I said. "And it takes time to remember things sometimes."

"Oooof," someone groaned. "Let's get on with it."

"Maria Theresa Asmar was born in Telkaif," I continued, "but she lived much of her childhood in Baghdad, where her family moved because of unrest in her hometown. It was in Baghdad that she grew up, received an education, started a girl's school, and began developing into the writer and woman we remember today."

The group nodded as we moved to the next display. It featured a dark suit and tie, a leather briefcase, and a photo of a man with slicked-back hair and thick glasses.

"This," I began, pointing to the photograph, "is Tareq Aziz. He was one of the most prominent Chaldean politicians in Iraq's history."

"Was he the guy who was friends with Saddam Hussein?" Zaya asked, narrowing his eyes at the photo.

"Well, he worked for him," I said. "Tareq Aziz served as Iraq's Deputy Prime Minister and Foreign Minister during the 1980s and 1990s. He was the public face of Iraq on the international stage, meeting with world leaders and negotiating during some of the country's most turbulent times."

"How did he get into politics?" Mary asked, her pen poised over her notebook.

"Tareq Aziz was born in Tel Keppe on April 28, 1936," I explained. "He studied English literature at Baghdad University and started his career as a journalist. Over time, he became involved in politics and joined the Baath Party, which eventually brought him into Saddam Hussein's inner circle."

Zaya hesitated before asking, "Was he… a good guy or a bad guy?"

"It's complicated," I said, pausing to let the weight of the question settle. "You see, what people outside of Iraq don't know is that most people *had to* join the Baath Party to get jobs or even enter college. As Christians, Chaldeans were already a persecuted minority, and not being Baathist created even more serious problems for them."

"Did your family have to join the Bath Party?" a kid asked.

The children in chorus corrected him, "It's Baath!" He had difficulty picking out the pronunciation and they tried to provide lessons but soon the museum sounded like it was run by sheep saying, "Baaaa, Baaaa…"

"Alright, enough of these shenanigans," Mr. Yatooma stepped in. "Let Ms. Weam move on."

"Thank you, Mr. Yatooma," I said, "and to answer the earlier question, no we did not join the Baath Party. Luckily, my family left Iraq before the situation got worse."

The group listened intently as I continued. "Most Iraqi Baathists paid a membership fee just to keep the government off their backs. They didn't participate in any of Saddam's brutalities. As for Tareq Aziz, by being in the government, he was able to help safeguard his people and Christians in general. It's likely because of his presence that Saddam allowed Christians to practice their faith and maintain their cultural traditions."

"So, he was kind of protecting his community?" Lola asked.

"Yes," I said. "But he wasn't just a passive observer. Tareq Aziz was admired for his intelligence and diplomatic skills. He was instrumental in presenting Iraq's position to the world during major conflicts, like the Iran-Iraq War and the Gulf War. At the same time, he was part of a regime that committed serious human rights abuses. His legacy is controversial, and people have different opinions about him. What's undeniable is that he played a significant role in shaping Iraq's modern history."

The group stood in reflective silence for a moment, taking in the complexity of his story. They then made their way to a display featuring a list of notable figures associated with Baghdad. The names were etched onto a sleek plaque, accompanied by portraits and brief descriptions.

Mary pointed at my name on the plaque and turned to me with astonishment.

"Ms. Weam, that's your name!" she exclaimed.

"Of course, her name would be there!" Mr. Yatooma said. "She was born in Baghdad, and she's the author of the first Chaldean American novel, *The Feminine Art*, and the creator of the first Iraqi American feature narrative, *Pomegranate*."

The children began chatting amongst themselves, nodding approvingly, as if I wasn't standing right there. I felt my cheeks grow warm and I waved my hands slightly, trying to downplay the attention, but Mr. Yatooma wasn't finished. He listed the global awards my work received, such as an Eric Hoffer Award and from Francis Coppola's Zoetrope.

"Mr. Yatooma," I said, starting to interrupt, but he kept going.

"She's been a strong advocate for preserving Chaldean culture and history," he continued, "and she's only started…"

"Thank you, Mr. Yatooma," I said, now fully red in the face. "But let's move on to the others…"

"But as their teacher, I have to tell them who's who!" he insisted.

"I think they get the picture," I said.

The kids glanced at me with a mix of admiration and excitement, and for a moment, I could sense how much it meant to them to see someone from their community achieve such recognition. When I was their age, I had no one to look to who represented my heritage in this way.

"Let's keep going," I said, leading the group toward the next gallery. Their laughter and excitement followed me, a reminder that even as we honor the past, we are shaping the future.

CHAPTER 10

Beyond Baghdad

The lights dimmed as we entered the final chapter of our journey. The sign *Beyond Baghdad* greeted us, and I gave it a nod in return. A sprawling map covered the wall, twisting like the branches of a very old tree. Cities like Mosul, Basra, Kirkuk, and Erbil glowed with golden markers, scattered like stars in the night.

"Baghdad is just one chapter of the big picture," I said, turning to the group. "Chaldeans have left their mark far beyond this city, shaping the history and culture of these lands for centuries."

Zaya's eyes locked onto Mosul's glowing marker. "That's where my grandpa's family is from!" he said, his voice brimming with pride as he traced the distance between it and Baghdad with his finger.

"Mine too," added Lola. "But they left a long time ago."

"That's where Elias al-Musili's family was from too," I said. "Remember him? Unfortunately, many

Chaldeans have had to leave these cities due to conflict and persecution. But before we get into that, let's dive into the history of these places."

I pointed to a photo of Mosul's skyline, its iconic churches rising above the city. "Mosul was once a major center of Chaldean life. It's home to the Chaldean Catholic Archeparchy of Mosul and the historic Church of Our Lady of Perpetual Help, also known as *Um al-Mauna*. This church is over eighty years old and was heavily damaged during ISIS's occupation of Mosul. The militants destroyed Christian symbols, wrote propaganda on its walls, and even used the church as a religious police office."

The group leaned in to look at a photo of the beautifully restored church, its white walls gleaming in the sunlight. "But," I continued, "with the support of donations, the church was rebuilt and consecrated in 2024. It's more than a building—it's a symbol of faith and resilience."

As I spoke, I noticed that, once again, the group's energy was waning. One boy was standing up asleep, teetering back and forth like a spinning top about to fall. Another child leaned against the wall, his head drooping. And Mary—poor Mary—was sitting on the floor, her head tilted back, snoring softly, her notebook sitting on her lap.

I blinked in disbelief, then glanced at Mr.

Yatooma. He caught my eye, chortled, and whispered, "Let me handle this."

He stepped forward, clapping his hands loudly. "Alright, troops! Time to wake up! You've made it this far, and trust me, you'll *want* to hear this part. Who's ready for some Yatooma magic?"

The kids perked up, startled but curious.

"Here's the deal," he said. "Whoever stays awake and alert for the rest of the tour will get special homemade *taghratha* that you will eat your fingers after."

The children cheered.

"Alright, now, Ms. Weam, take over."

Relieved, I strode over to the next panel, a photo of Basra's port. "Let's move on to Basra, a port city in southern Iraq. It is home to the Chaldean Catholic Church of Saint Thomas. My cousins were born and raised there, and let me tell you, those Basrawis know how to make kleicha—the best date cookies you'll ever eat!"

Zaya raised his hand. "Can we have *kleicha* if we're good today?"

"What, you think this is a restaurant?" Mr. Yatooma asked.

"Or your mom's kitchen?" John asked, laughing, and others threw in their comments of "or your aunt's or grandmother's or…" the list went on and on.

"Enough!" Helen bellowed and everyone stopped

in their tracks. "Let's let Ms. Weam complete the tour."

She really placed some fear into them as they behaved like perfect angels afterward. I took advantage of this moment to move to the next display, featuring Kirkuk's Sacred Heart Cathedral and the ruins of the Mother of Sorrows Cathedral.

"What's this karaoke?" one kid asked trying to read the sign.

"It's Kirkuk," I said, as some of the children burst into laughter. "It's an oil-rich city with a deep Chaldean history. In it, there's the 'Red Church,' a shrine built to honor martyrs who died for their faith."

"What's the Red Church?" asked Lola, twirling her hair.

"The Red Church is named after a Persian officer, Tahmazgerd, who was involved in a massacre of Christians in 445 A.D. under King Yazdegerd II."

"A massacre?" Mary asked, her voice solemn.

"Yes," I said. "During this tragedy, 12,000 Christians, including clergy, were killed for refusing to renounce their faith. But the story doesn't end there. Tahmazgerd, the officer ordered to carry out the massacre, was so moved by the victims' unwavering faith that he converted to Christianity. For this, he was executed at the same site, becoming a martyr himself."

The group stared at me in stunned silence.

"To honor the martyrs," I continued, "a shrine for martyrs was built on the hill around 470 A.D. It became known as the 'Red Church,' most likely because of the blood of the martyrs."

"That's so sad," Mary said.

"It is," I said. "The Red Church and the Mother of Sorrows Cathedral remind us of the sacrifices made to preserve our faith and identity."

The group fell quiet, lost in reflection.

Finally, we stopped at a vibrant photo of Ankawa, the Christian suburb of Erbil. "And this," I said, "is Ankawa. It's become a haven for Chaldeans displaced from other parts of Iraq. They're rebuilding their lives here, creating schools, businesses, and even a university. This is resilience in action."

As we wrapped up the tour, Zaya raised his hand. "So basically, Chaldeans are everywhere, but they've had a really hard time."

"That's one way to put it," I said.

"But the key takeaway," Mr. Yatooma interjected, "is that Chaldeans are unstoppable. No matter where they go, they preserve their culture, faith, and traditions. And they don't just survive—they thrive."

"Even with all the moving around, they've stayed strong," Mary said, now fully awake.

"They have," Mr. Yatooma said. "And who knows? Maybe one of you will be the next Chaldean GOAT."

"Are you calling the children goats?" asked Helen, astonished.

"Greatest of All Time," Zaya explained, as the group giggled, some laughing so hard they held their stomachs.

"Isn't there goat cheese too?" someone else asked.

"Yes," I said with a chuckle. "Now, before we get too far into the topic of food, let's go eat and celebrate."

"Yes!" the kids cheered, their earlier fatigue forgotten.

As we headed toward the exit, I overheard some of the children excitedly planning to share what they'd learned with their parents. It warmed my heart to know that these stories, like the caravans of old and the airplanes of today, would journey far beyond the museum's walls, carrying the richness of Iraq's heritage to new places and hearts.

The End

YOUR TURN TO EXPLORE!

1. Storytellers of Baghdad
   - Ask your family if they've visited Baghdad or know stories about it.
   - Write your own short story inspired by city life.

2. Map Your Baghdad
   - Create a map of Baghdad or another city connected to your family.
   - Add landmarks and places that are meaningful or famous.

3. Baghdad Time Capsule
   - Gather photos, items, or drawings about Baghdad.
   - Write a letter explaining why they matter and seal them in a time capsule.

4. Traditions Keeper
   - Ask about a tradition from Baghdad or Iraqi culture.
   - Recreate it—cook a dish, make a craft, or celebrate a holiday.

5. City Voices
   - Record or write down a family member's memories of Baghdad.
   - Share what you've learned through art, writing, or a video.

CONTINUE THE JOURNEY

Want to explore more stories about our ancient heritage and modern adventures? Here are some books you might enjoy:

- The Magical Museum Series
- Little Baghdad
- Pomegranate (also available as a movie)
- Mesopotamian Goddesses
- Iraqi American Series: The Lives of the Artists

You can find these books on Amazon or visit www.weamnamou.com to discover more stories!

Other Great Books About Chaldean History and Culture:

Visit your local library or bookstore to discover more wonderful books about Chaldean history and culture! You can also ask your teachers and family members to help you find age-appropriate books about our rich heritage.

ABOUT ME, YOUR MUSEUM GUIDE AND CHALDEAN STORYTELLER!

I was born in Baghdad, Iraq as a Chaldean—we're Christian Catholics also known as Neo-Babylonians, and yes, we still speak Aramaic, the language Jesus spoke! When I was your age, just ten years old, my family and I moved to Michigan in the United States. Did you know Michigan has the largest population of Chaldeans in the whole world?

People call me the Chaldean Storyteller because I've been writing stories for almost as long as I can remember. Stories help us understand who we are and where we came from, and I've written nearly two dozen books so far! I've also made two movies that have won over forty awards. Sometimes

I still can't believe that the little girl who moved from Baghdad grew up to tell stories that people all around the world want to hear.

I speak three languages—English, Arabic, and Aramaic—and I love to travel and learn about different cultures. I studied writing in college and even learned poetry in a beautiful city called Prague! When I'm not writing or producing films, I'm spending time with my two beautiful children, my husband, and our lovable dog who always makes us laugh.

In 2019, I began an exciting journey when I became the executive director of the Chaldean Cultural Center. That's where you'll find the world's first and only Chaldean Museum—the very one you've just visited through this book.

As a writer and filmmaker, I feel so honored to create stories that touch people's hearts and to share our incredible history with young people like you. Every time I tell someone about our past, I'm not just teaching them history—I'm helping them discover pieces of themselves they never knew existed.